Pumpkintown
The Haunted Hayride

BY Peggy Schaedler

ILLUSTRATIONS BY Sarah Rawson Fris

TURTLE HILL BOOKS

For Joe, who loves Halloween, pumpkins and palm trees.
—P.S

For Grammy and Grampy Rawson, who have always supported my creative dreams.
—S.F.

Turtle Hill Books
Venice, FL 34293
Visit us at www.turtlehillbooks.com

Illustrations: Sarah Rawson Fris
Peggy Schaedler author photo: Kim Tyler Photography, KTPhoto.net
Cover and interior design: Ashley Scott, Ashleyscottdesigns.com

Publisher's Cataloging-In-Publication Data
(Prepared by The Donohue Group, Inc.)

Names: Schaedler, Peggy, author. | Fris, Sarah Rawson, illustrator.
Title: Pumpkintown. The haunted hayride / by Peggy Schaedler ; illustrated by Sarah Rawson Fris.
Other Titles: Haunted hayride
Description: Venice, FL : Turtle Hill Books, [2021] | Interest age level: 005-010. | Summary: "Ned must find a way to overcome his Halloween fears so he can join his friends on Pumpkintown's haunted hayride"-- Provided by publisher.
Identifiers: ISBN 9780989819565 (hardback) | ISBN 9780989819572 (paperback)
Subjects: LCSH: Pumpkin--Juvenile fiction. | Hayrides--Juvenile fiction. | Fear--Juvenile fiction. | Friendship--Juvenile fiction. | Halloween--Juvenile fiction. | CYAC: Pumpkin--Fiction. | Hayrides--Fiction. | Fear--Fiction. | Friendship--Fiction. | Halloween--Fiction.
Classification: LCC PZ7.S33147 Puh 2020 | DDC [E]--dc23

This book was typeset in Plantin Infant MT Std.

It was the week before Halloween. But the pumpkin pals weren't thinking about costumes or candy. They were excited about something else.

"Did you hear about the Haunted Hayride on Halloween night?" Phil asked.
"I heard there are monsters, witches and ghosts," Meadow said.
"Did you say g-g-ghosts?" Ned stuttered.
"Spooktacular!" Phil laughed.

Ned didn't laugh. He felt a chill.
His heart pounded. His teeth chattered.

Ned remembered last Halloween.
He saw dark doorsteps and flickering faces.
Shadows slinked behind big scary trees.

"Gotcha!" a witch shouted.
"Grrrrr," a monster growled.
"BOO!" a ghost jumped out.

"Ned, your cheeks look yellow," said Meadow.
"You're not scared, are you?" Phil asked.
"No way," said Ned. "I'm like Squash Gourdon. Nothing scares me."
But Ned's voice squeaked. His legs wobbled like Jell-O.

"It's time for Halloween math," Miss Pearberry announced. "Neddington Patch, what is five ghosts minus two?"

"Oh, boy, oh boy, oh boy," Ned muttered. His knees knocked together. "Um, um," Ned stuttered.

"Three!" Phil shouted. "Phil Cider, next time please raise your hand," said Miss Pearberry.

When Ned got home, he stuffed his book in the dishwasher and a glass in his backpack.

He tossed Sassy's food in the washing machine and his stinky socks in her bowl.

Mommo found Ned's crayons in her purse. Ned was coloring with her lipstick. "Oh, picklesticks," said Mommo.

At bedtime, Daddo said, "Son, your brain has turned to mush."

"Oh, Daddo," Ned wailed. "On Halloween, my whole class is going on the haunted hayride."

"That sounds fun. What's the problem?"

"I'm afraid of monsters, witches — and especially ghosts!"

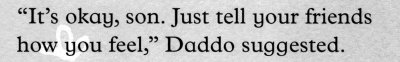

"It's okay, son. Just tell your friends how you feel," Daddo suggested.

"What if they make fun of me?" Ned cried.

"You don't have to go on the ride if you don't want to," Daddo said.
"But I want to go."
"You *don't* want to go, but you *do* want to go?"
"WAH!" Ned pulled the blanket over his head.

"This is a conundrum," Daddo said.
"A what?"
"That means a tough problem," Daddo replied. "Can I join you under there?"
Ned sniffed, "I guess."

"When I was little, I was afraid of riding a bike," Daddo explained.
"That's a funny thing to be afraid of," Ned said.
"I know. But it wasn't funny then."

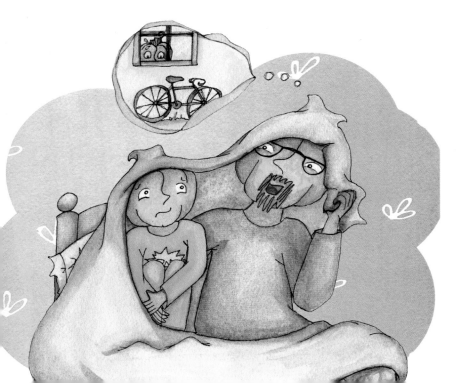

"What did you do?"
Ned asked.

Daddo thought
for a minute.

"I asked for help. I
knew my true friends
wouldn't laugh at me."

Ned hiccupped. Then he tooted.
Daddo laughed. "Can we come out now?"

It was Halloween night.
"This is going to be awesome!" Meadow squealed.
"Spooktacular!" shouted Phil.

Ned sighed, "I'm not going."
"Why not?" Phil asked.
Ned took a deep breath.
"I'm afraid."

Ghostly howls drifted through the woods.
Meadow gasped. "What was that?"
An owl hooted in the distance.
"Ned, I'm scared, too," Phil admitted.

"Then let's stick together," said Meadow.
"And close our eyes when we get to the creepy parts," Phil added.

"Don't forget Sassy!" Daddo grinned. "She likes a fun fright too!"

They piled onto the hay wagon.
Chili Pepper shouted, "Giddy-up, Strawtail!"
With a bounce and a bump, the wagon
lurched forward.
Clip-clop, clip-clop.

"Here we go," Ned whispered.

Bats squeaked as they bobbed up and down.
Eek, eek, eek! The pals huddled together.
Clip-clop, clip-clop.

A witch cackled as she rocked on her broom.
Hee-hee-hee! The pals
held hands.
Clip-clop, clip-clop.

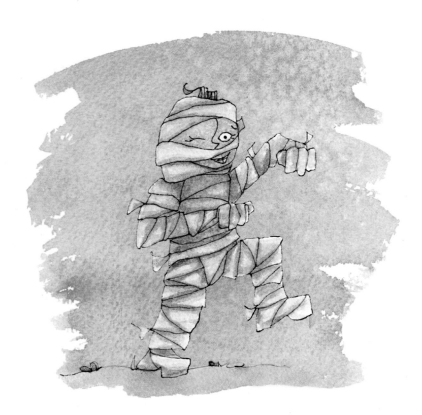

A mummy moaned as it stomped the ground.
O-o-o-o-ahhhh!

The pals closed their eyes.
Clip-clop, clip-clop.

Then the wagon stopped right in front of — the ghosts!
Who-o-o-o-o!
Ned squeezed his eyes extra tight.
"Oh boy, oh boy, oh boy!"
His teeth chattered so hard, he could barely speak.

"Ned, look! It's Miss Pearberry!" cried Meadow.

"Whooooo ghosts there?" their teacher moaned.

"And Lucy Lemon, the librarian," said Phil.

"Check out my boo-k!" Lucy smiled.

Ned opened his eyes.

"Happy Halloween!" said Fire Chief Marley Melon.

Postman Pete Beet said, "You know me, kids. I work at the *ghost* office!"
Glenn Gazpacho took a night off from the barbershop.
"Don't we look boo-tiful?" Halloween music began playing.
"Let's boo-gie!" Lucy said.
The pals laughed, danced and sang songs.

"Time to move on!" Chili Pepper announced.
"Giddy-up, Strawtail!"
With a bounce and a bump, the wagon lurched forward.
Clip-clop, clip-clop.

The pals huddled together.
But this time they kept their eyes open.

A black cat hissed.
It was fluffy.

A skeleton rattled.
It dangled from strings.

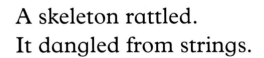

A monster groaned.
But it was just cardboard.

The ride ended. "We made it!" the friends cheered.
They hopped off the wagon.
Phil said, "C'mon, Ned. Let's go trick or treating!"

But Ned was nowhere in sight.
"Ned?" Daddo called. "Where are you?"
The wind whistled. The moon glowed.

"BOO!" Ned jumped out from behind a tree.

"Yikes!" Daddo laughed.

"This is the best Halloween ever," Meadow said.

"Spooktacular!" Phil added.

"Time to go," Daddo said. "Ready, gang?"

"Daddo, I already know my costume for next year," Ned grinned.
"Really? What's that?"
"A ghost!"

Daddo smiled. "That's the spirit."

Peggy Schaedler was a school librarian before becoming a writer. She is the author of the Dagger and Dash series, *Pumpkintown: The Great Goose Getaway, Pumpkin Palooza* and "Sassy's Song." Peggy loves fun books that make children smile. She continues to write stories, plays, and poetry for children while her sugar pumpkin doggie tries to distract her. When Peggy is not writing, she performs in Puppets 4 Peace, where she reads, sings and plays her ukulele in schools and libraries.

Visit Peggy at www.turtlehillbooks.com and www.puppets4peace.net.

Sarah Rawson Fris is the illustrator of the new Pumpkintown book series including *The Great Goose Getaway* and *Pumpkin Palooza*. She has had a great passion for drawing, painting and telling stories for as long as she can remember. She lives in Beverly, Massachusetts with her husband and little sweetie pumpkin Eva. When she is not painting, she can be found biking, baking or exploring the rocky shores of Maine and dreaming about blueberries. She and her husband make whimsical onesies and wall hangings in their spare time.

Visit Sarah at www.sarahrawsonfris.com and www.turtlehillbooks.com.

Made in the USA
Columbia, SC
17 June 2023

17900217R00020